This book belongs to

For
Teddy, Babby, Bruno
and the gang.

To

....

with love from

....

Written by Katherine Sully
Illustrated by Janet Samuel
Designed by Chris Fraser at Page to Page

This edition published by Parragon in 2011

Parragon
Queen Street House
4 Queen Street
Bath BA1 1HE, UK

ISBN 978-1-4454-3467-4

Printed in China

Where, Oh Where Is Huggle Buggle Bear?

PaRragon

Bath • New York • Singapore • Hong Kong • Cologne • Delhi
Melbourne • Amsterdam • Johannesburg • Auckland • Shenzhen

Where, oh where is **Huggle Buggle** Bear?
I can't find him anywhere!
He always hides when it's time for bed.
He is such a **funny** bear!

Is he snacking on toast and honey,
Making crumbs with **Babbity Bunny**?

No!
He isn't with
Babbity Bunny.

Huggle Buggle knows it's bedtime
But this happens every night!
I can't go to bed without him.
It just would not be right.

Where, oh where is **Huggle Buggle** Bear?
I can't find him anywhere!
He always hides when it's time for bed.
He is such a **silly** bear!

Is he bouncing on his belly,
On the sofa with Ellie Nellie?

No!
He isn't bouncing with
Ellie Nellie.
And he isn't snacking with
Babbity Bunny.

It's way past **Huggle Buggle**'s bedtime
And I'm starting to feel sleepy.
I can't go to bed without him,
It's much too dark and creepy.

Where, oh where is **Huggle Buggle** Bear?
I can't find him anywhere!
He always hides when it's time for bed.
He is such a **naughty** bear!

Is he making lots of noise
With **Woolly Lamb** and the other toys?

No!
He isn't playing with
Woolly Lamb.
He isn't bouncing with
Ellie Nellie.
He isn't snacking with
Babbity Bunny.

It's way past **Huggle Buggle**'s bedtime
And I'm feeling worried now.
I can't go to bed without him.
I don't think that I know how.

Where, oh where is **Huggle Buggle** Bear?
I can't find him anywhere!
He always hides when it's time for bed.
He is such a **troublesome** bear.

Is he splashing in the tub,
Blowing bubbles with Rubadub?

No!

He isn't splashing with
Rubadub.
He isn't playing with
Woolly Lamb.
He isn't bouncing with
Ellie Nellie.
He isn't snacking with
Babbity Bunny.

It's way past **Huggle Buggle**'s bedtime
And now I'm feeling sad.
I don't want to go to bed without him,
It would make me feel so bad!

I know where...
there's Huggle Buggle Bear!
And here are all the other toys.
I think they must be fast asleep,
So, **sssh!** Don't make any noise!

Night-night!